2-rabbit, 7-wind

TONI DE GEREZ

2-RABBIT, 7-WIND

Poems from Ancient Mexico
Retold from Nahuatl Texts

The Viking Press   New York

First Edition

Copyright © 1971 by Toni de Gerez · All rights reserved
First published in 1971 by The Viking Press, Inc.
625 Madison Avenue, New York, N.Y. 10022
Published simultaneously in Canada by
The Macmillan Company of Canada Limited
Library of Congress catalog card number: 77-136829
Printed in U.S.A.
1 2 3 4 5 75 74 73 72 71

898   1. Mexico—poetry
2. Poetry—ancient Mexico
VLB 670-73688-0
670-73687-2

Illustrations from *Design Motifs of Ancient Mexico* by Jorge Enciso,
Dover Publications, Inc., New York. Reprinted through permission
of the publisher.

Author's Note

The word *Nahua* means "one who speaks with
authority." The Nahuatl-speaking people were a
chosen people with the special right to make god-
poems, praise-poems. The Nahuatl of these
poems is not the language spoken today, the
language of everyday affairs. It is the language of
the wise men and the shamans of long ago. These
are the words from the *xochicalli*, the house-of-
songs-house-of-flowers.

Amoxtli—the books as sources
It is generally believed that two hundred years
before Christ a Nahuatl-speaking culture had
been well established in the high plateaus of
Mexico. In their magic books, "the picture
books," the Nahuas recorded the sacred hap-
penings. These "picture books" were folded
sheets of paper made from the bark of the *amatl*,
a wild fig tree, or from deerskin or maguey. The

6 sheets were folded in such a way that they could be opened like a screen. They were usually about sixteen feet long and about seven inches wide. Bernal Díaz del Castillo, a soldier and a chronicler of the Spanish Conquest, described the houses and schools and temples where the wise men guarded "the many books of paper folded like Castilian clothes."

In Mexico-Tenochtitlán there were many kinds of schools, but the best known were the *telpochcalli,* or houses for young people, and the *calmecac,* or centers of higher learning. The old hymns, poems, and historical events were all learned by heart.

Bernardino de Sahagún, a Franciscan monk and historian, described the method of instruction used by the wise men. "They taught them to sing all the verses of the songs which are called divine. The verses were written in their books with characters. . . . They also taught them Indian astrology, the meaning of dreams, and the count of years."

The first attempts to preserve native literary texts date from the sixteenth century. Fray

Andrés de Olmos, who arrived in New Spain in
1528, collected a great number of orations delivered by the wise men and the elders. These texts
are known as *huehuetlatolli.* They were the discourses made on important occasions such as the
death of a king, the election of a new governor,
or the birth of a royal child. The texts also include the advice of the elders to their children—
words to a son, words to a daughter.

More important than the work of Olmos was
the research undertaken by Sahagún. With the
help of native students of the colleges of Tlatelolco, Tepepulco, and Mexico City, Sahagún began collecting hundreds of texts. The students
wrote down the narratives of the Indian elders,
using the Latin alphabet. This material served
as the basis for the monumental work, *Historia
general de las cosas de Nueva España.* These
Nahuatl texts have been preserved in three codices, two in Madrid and one in Florence.

Another important manuscript is *El libro de
los colloquios.* Here is recorded a dramatic encounter which took place in the courtyard of the
San Francisco monastery in Mexico City in 1524,

8 a confrontation between the first twelve mission- ary friars who came to New Spain and the Nahuatl-speaking elders and wise men, who de- fended their way of thinking and their gods. Part of the *Colloquio*, as it is called, is included in this book, pages 51–56.

The leading pioneer work in Nahuatl and Nahuatl literature was done by the great Mexi- can scholar and priest, Dr. Angel María Garibay. His most important works include his Nahuatl grammar, *Llave de Nahuatl,* and his many vol- umes of translations into Spanish of the Sahagún books. Since Dr. Garibay's death in 1967 his work has been carried on brilliantly by Dr. Miguel León-Portilla. He has written many stud- ies of the ancient Nahuatl world and its philoso- phy and mythology. Special acknowledgment must be made here to his vast knowledge and scholarship.

Quetzalcoatl—the gods
Nahuatl poetry has to be read within a frame- work of the many gods and the 1-god. Their names are beautiful and are poems in themselves.

Though the Aztecs had a concept of a god with the name *Tloque Nahuaque Ipalnemohuani Yohualli Ehecatl,* which means Lord-master-of-the-near-and-far-giver-of-life-night-and-wind, they also had Quetzalcoatl. Who was Quetzalcoatl? There is the god and there is the historical priest-king who lived in Tollan (Tula) at the height of the Toltec civilization, during the years dating from *1-ree d* (A.D. 947). This Quetzalcoatl taught his people the arts of writing, drawing, metal working, and making polychrome polished pottery. To be a Toltec was "to be an artist." He abolished human sacrifice and taught that the only offerings to the gods should be tortillas, flowers, incense, and butterflies and snakes.

The legendary god Quetzalcoatl has many names. He is known also as Ehecatl, wind-god-cloud-serpent. He is the god of learning. He is the god of agriculture, and he discovered the most sacred of all food, corn. He is the god of the planet Venus.

According to the codices, "It is said . . . in [the year] 2-rabbit Quetzalcoatl arrived in Tula where he built his house of penance . . . it is said. . . . "

10   And the sign of Quetzalcoatl in the ancient count of days is 7-wind. Every man as well as the gods was born under a particular sign. His destiny was controlled by his sign. Even today in Mexico they say, "Every man has his own rabbit."

These poems are no more than shapes-of-poems, workings from Sahagún, Garibay and León-Portilla. They should be read as parts of one long poem, a poem that does not begin anywhere and does not end anywhere. A line can be chosen to be repeated over and over until its burden has been exhausted. It should be remembered that these words formed part of a ritual dance and ceremony, of something-sacred-that-was-going-on. Just as the first tree of the world, the ceiba, grows in the exact center of the earth, these poems find their center in the earth and in the body of man. These poems cannot be separated from the situation in which the poems were *first* sung or chanted.

Unfortunately we cannot go back to this *first*. We cannot dance the poem. We cannot be the poem. Or can we?

Mexico-Tenochtitlán   T. DE G.

2-rabbit, 7-wind

Listen!
I am the singer
   I am singing
the pictures of the book
I am the blue-and-green
    bird
I make the codices speak
I am the quetzal

What is my song?
my song is a piece of
    jade
I cut into it
it is my song
look how I string beads of jade
    into a necklace
it is my song
it is my jade song

As quetzal feathers
beautiful is my song
look how my song
bends down over the earth
in the house of butterflies my song
    is born

16

Listen!
I am the singer   I am lord-firefly
I wander over water-lily pools
my wings
      gold-streaked
beside the *teponaztle**   beside the *huehuetle*†
beside the drums

Teponaztle: a drum made of a hollow piece of wood. Still used today.
†*Huehuetle:* a drum made of wood or of clay. Still used today.

O my heart you must be strong
love the sunflower
    the flower
    of the 1-god

are we here on earth for nothing?
    the sunflower fades
    the sunflower dies
I fade
I die

18

I coyote-hungry-for-wisdom I say:
we are only a little while here
not forever on earth not forever on earth
only a little while
　　though it is jade it will be broken
　　though it is gold it will be crushed
　　though it is quetzal feather
　　it will be torn apart
not forever on earth not forever on earth
only a little while

Who will know my name?
    at least my songs?
    at least my flowers?
what is there to do?
are we here on earth for nothing?
    at least my songs
    at least my flowers

My song understands
    I stop
    I listen
I look at a flower
    o do not fade away
    o do not fade away

Yollotl my heart
what are you up to?
you are a thief
catch the black-and-red water
catch it in your word-net
and make a song

I hear
the words of the *coyolli* bird
    he is answering the 1-god

his words
rain down
like jade
his words
rain down
like quetzal
feathers

is this what pleases the 1-god?
    is this real?
    is this real?
is this the way?

Do we have roots?
are we real?

o-great-inventor
o-greatest-god-who-is-inventor-of-himself:
    we are sad
    we must leave things
      unfinished
    we must go away
on earth: flowers-and-song
    let us rejoice
    let us live
on earth: flowers-and-song

24

I am a fish
in the swamp grass
I sigh
how I long to sing

o-great-lord-and-high-prince-of-the-turtles
I beg you
I want to be like my brothers
    the water-beetle
    the hornet
    the bumblebee
how lovely their songs are
and the song of the green frog
    who answers from his home
    on the lentil leaf

I am golden
but I have no song
the turtledove has gold bells
    in his throat

I cry out
o-god-of-the-near-and-far
am I not one of your creatures?
    the sandfish
    the minnow

I want to speak
I want to sing

Look!
the eagle and tiger princes
are dressing themselves
for war

they are copper-and-gold birds
  guacamayas
now they are green-and-black thrushes
now they are red parrots

the princes are wearing garlands of wild clover

there is glory
  in war songs
  in war flowers
the sacred water
the sacred fire
are refreshed with tassels of blood

Are you afraid Prince Tlacahuepan?*
are you trembling?
you are going to make your home
where-all-is-joy

your face is painted with marl
you are wearing a cape of hummingbird
    feathers
shoulders of princes carry you as you go
to the place-of-mystery
shields are clashing
kettle drums are beating
the juice of cocoa is drunk

are you trembling?
are you afraid Prince Tlacahuepan?

*Prince Tlacahuepan (d. 1495–98): brother of King Moctezuma II.

O-mother-of-the-gods
o-father-of-the-gods
    I speak to you!

oldest-god-of-the-jade-navel-of-the-earth
mother-and-father-and-oldest god
    I speak to you!

lord-of-the-fire and lord-of-the-years
your house is in waters bluebird color
your house is in the clouds
your house is in the
    dark
    difficult
country of the dead
    I speak to you!

30 lady-of-the-starry-skirt
lady-of-the-jade-petticoat
    lady-of-our-flesh
    lord-of-our-flesh
she-who-makes-the-earth-solid
he-who-covers-the-earth-with-cotton
    I speak to you!

I direct my words
toward the place-of-duality
above the 9-levels-of-heaven
    I speak to you!

Where is the house of quetzal feathers?
where is the house of turquoise?
where is the house of shells?

in Tollan*
in Tollan
　　o ay!

but our lord Quetzalcoatl has
　　vanished
he has gone to Tlapallan
to the red-and-black country
　　o ay!

*Tollan: sacred Toltec city, known today as Tula.

In Tollan they say
there were birds rare and beautiful
small birds the color of
    turquoise
birds with green-and-yellow
    feathers
and yellow birds with breasts
    fire-color
    flame-color
and all sang in the name of our prince
o Nactitl
    o ay!
    o ay!

In Tollan   squashes
were round and heavy as drums
   and gold as morning

an ear of corn
was as big as the great tongue
of the *metlatl**
   the yellow corn
   the red corn
   the dark corn
and one ear was all a man could carry

amaranth leaves were as big
   as palm fronds
you could climb up on them

**Metlatl:* the stone on which corn and chocolate are ground.

34 and cotton grew on the bushes
    in balls of every color
    blue and green and red and yellow

    in Tollan
    in Tollan
            o ay!
            o ay!
    our lord Quetzalcoatl has
        vanished

The Toltecs were wise
they conversed with their own hearts

they played their drums
they played their rattles
    they were singers
    they made songs
the Toltecs guarded the songs
in their memories

the Toltecs were wise
they conversed with their own hearts

The true artist is a *tlacuilo*
he paints with red-and-black ink
with black water
the true artist is wise
god is in his heart   he paints god
      into things
he knows all colors
he makes shapes   he draws feet
      and faces
he paints shadows
he is a Toltec
he has a dialogue with his own heart

The true storyteller is a *tlaquetzqui*
he says things boldly
with the lips and mouth of an artist
the true storyteller uses words of joy
flowers are on his lips
his language is strict
his language is noble

the bad storyteller is careless
he confuses words   he swallows them
he says useless words
he has no dignity

The true doctor is a *tlamatini*
he is a wise man   he gives life
he knows herbs   stones   trees   roots
he examines   he experiments   he sets bones
he gives potions   he bleeds his patients
he cuts and sews   he stops the bleeding
with ashes

Ear-of-corn
you are a copper bell
you are a fruit pit
you are a sea shell
    white   white
you are crystal
    white   white

you are a green stone
you are a bracelet
you are precious
you are our flesh
you are our bones

0-7-ears-of-corn
    awake!
    awake!
you are our mother
    arise now!
do not leave us orphans
do not leave us orphans

go now
to Tlaloc's rain-house
to Tlaloc's mist-house

Tlaloc-the-rain-god
Tlaloc-of-foam-sandals
Tlaloc-of-thunder-rattles
    go to him!

My son
listen to our words with good judgment
look at things
look long and wisely   ask yourself
    what is real?
    what is true?
that is how you must work and act

42 in a secret place the elders
          the-wrinkled-faces-and-the-white-hair
     left us these words:
     look long and wisely   ask yourself
          what is real?
          what is true?

     listen to their words
          Listen!

          my son
     you will act
     you will cut wood
     you will work the land
          you will plant cactus
          you will sow maguey
     you will have drink
     you will have food
     you will have clothing
     you will grow straight
          and tall
     you will be spoken of with praise

one day
you will tie yourself to a
    skirt-and-blouse
what will she have to eat?
what will she have to drink?
will she live on air?

you are her support
    you are the eagle
    you are the tiger

    My daughter
my necklace of precious stones
you are my blood
you are my color
you are my image
    now listen!
    now understand!
you are alive
you have been born
Nopiltzin our lord has sent you to earth

here on earth there is
    heartache
    worry
    fatigue
a wind blows
    it is obsidian
    it is sharp
    it is cold
we are burned by the sun
we are burned by the wind

but our lord has given us
    food
    sleep
he has given us strength
he has given us laughter

    my daughter
watch for the dawn
raise your face
raise your arms
    to the sky

wash your hands
cleanse your mouth

take up the broom
begin to sweep
    do not be idle
do not sit there close to the fire
help your little brothers

what else will you do?

46 you will prepare the food
you will prepare the drink
you will spin
you will weave
you will learn what is Toltec
        the art of feathers
        how to embroider in colors
        how to dye the threads

        my daughter
now listen!
now understand!

you are noble
you are precious
you are turquoise
you have been shaped by the gods

see that you do not dishonor them
do not act common
do not become ordinary

you are noble
you are precious
you are turquoise

    my daughter
pay attention
be strict with yourself

you were not meant to sell
    vegetables
    wood
    handfuls of *chilli*
    pots of salt
in the doorways of the houses
on the street

you are noble
you are turquoise

you will learn to spin
you will learn to weave
you will learn to prepare food and drink

48 you are not common
you must not cheapen yourself
you are not for every man
only to one give your love

choose your life companion with care
you must go to the end of life together
        do not leave him
        hold to him
even though he may be a poor man
        only a very small eagle
        only a very small tiger
do not neglect him

        my daughter
with these words
my duty is done

may the gods give you
a long and happy life
        my turquoise one

Cinteotl: I am corncob
I am streaked with red
I come from Tamoanchan

people: Cinteotl stands erect
Cinteotl is opening
god is here
the day-maker

Cinteotl: I am the god 1-flower
the most perfect of all
in the land-of-mist-and-rain

people: Cinteotl is singing
and the jaguar princes
are dancing
upon the mossy footstool of the
earth

50   here is the holy-seed ground
        the holy flower
      and the holy song
          to sing!
          to dance!

After the Spanish conquest, twelve missionary friars were sent to New Spain in 1524 to convert the ancient Nahuatl-speaking people to Christianity. The dramatic encounter between the friars and the elders and wise men is recorded in a famous manuscript, *El libro de los colloquios*. Here is a portion of it.

Our lords most esteemed most high
your journey has been hard and long
to reach this land

we who are humble
we who are ignorant
look at you

what is it that we should say?
what is it that your ears want to hear?
can there be meaning
in what we say to you?

52 we are common people
because of our god-of-the-near-and-far
because of him
we dare to speak
we exhale his breath and his words
      his air
for him and in his name
we dare to speak to you
despite the danger

perhaps we will be taken to our ruin
we are ordinary people
we can be killed
we can be destroyed
what are we to do?

allow us to die
let us perish now
since our gods are already dead

wait   be calm   our lords
we will break open
      a little

we will open
    a little
the secret of our god-who-is

you say
that we do not know
the right god
the god who owns the heavens
    and the earth

you say
our god is not a true god

we are disturbed
we are troubled by these words

our people
who lived upon the earth before us
did not speak
in this way
they taught us their way of life

54 the rules of worship
    and how to honor the gods
        to burn incense
        to offer sacrifices
    this is our way
    and the way of our ancestors

    they believed that the gods
    provide our sustenance
        all that we eat and drink
            corn
            beans
            amaranth
            sage
    therefore we pray
    to the gods for water
    and rain
    for the earth to be green
    and the gods give us courage
    and the ability
    to rule

for a long time it has been so
    at Tula
    at Huapalcalco
    at Xuchatlapan
    at Tlamohuanchan
    at Yohuallichan
    at Teotihuacán

and now must we destroy
the ancient order
    of the Chichimec?
    of the Toltec?
    of the Acolhua?
    of the Teopanec?

we know our god
he gives us life
he continues our race
we know how it is that we must pray

hear us   o lords
do not harm our people
do not destroy them
be calm and friendly
consider these matters   o lords

56 we cannot accept your words
we cannot accept your teachings as truth
even though this may offend you
we cannot agree
that our gods are wrong

is it not enough that we have already lost
that our way of life has been taken away?
is that not enough?

this is all we can say
this is our answer
to your words   o lords

do with us
as you please